AMABEL WILLIAMS-ELLIS

# THE ENCHANTED WORLD

## Part One

ILLUSTRATED BY
MOIRA KEMP

MACMILLAN CHILDREN'S BOOKS

*The Great White Cat, Childe Rowland, The Well of the World's End*
first published 1950 in *PRINCESSES AND TROLLS*

*Cap o' Rushes, The King, the Saint and the Goose,* and *White-Faced Siminy* first
published 1960 in *FAIRY TALES OF THE BRITISH ISLES*

*The Country of the Mice* and *The Magic Bird* first published 1966
in *OLD WORLD AND NEW WORLD FAIRY TALES*

*The Master Thief* first published in this compilation

This compilation first published in 1987 by
Hodder and Stoughton Children's Books

Picturemac edition published in 1988 by
MACMILLAN CHILDREN'S BOOKS
A division of Macmillan Publishers Limited
London and Basingstoke
Associated companies throughout the world

British Library Cataloguing in Publication Data
Williams-Ellis, Amabel, 1894-1984
    The enchanted world.
    Pt. 1
    I. Title        II. Kemp, Moira
    823'.914 [J]

    ISBN 0-333-48343-x

Designed by Annette Stachowiak

Printed in Hong Kong

# Contents

Foreword  5

Cap o' Rushes  6

The Great White Cat  15

Childe Rowland  22

The King, the Saint and the Goose  35

The Country of the Mice  42

The Well of the World's End  53

The Magic Bird  60

The Master Thief  75

White-Faced Siminy  94

illustrated by

MOIRA KEMP

*For my parents*

# Foreword

*A*MABEL WILLIAMS-ELLIS *was born into a literary family. Her father was St Loe Strachey, Editor of* The Spectator *for many years. She wrote many books for adults and children. She was fascinated by scientific developments until she died in 1984 at the age of 86. She was married to the well-known architect Sir Clough Williams-Ellis.*

*Lady Williams-Ellis will be best remembered for her story-telling. She travelled extensively and collected folk tales and legends from all the places she visited. She paid particular attention to local versions of stories and took a lot of trouble to find out as much as she could about sources and the history of the stories she collected.*

*Several collections were published including* Round the World Fairy Tales, Old World *and* New World Fairy Tales *and* Fairy Tales from the British Isles. *One of her aims was to help children to increase their understanding of countries other than their own.*

*The stories in this collection were chosen during the last year of Amabel's life. She included some old favourites as well as some less well-known but traditional tales. She aimed to give the greatest pleasure to the greatest possible number of her readers.*

# Cap o' Rushes

THERE WAS ONCE a very rich gentleman, and he had three daughters.

One day he thought he would like to see how fond they each were of him. So he says to the first:

'How much do you love me, my dear?'

'Why,' says she, 'I love you as I love my life.'

'That's good,' says he. So he says to the second, 'How much do you love me, dear daughter?'

'Why,' says she, 'I love you better than all the world.'

'That's good,' says he. So he says to the third, 'How much do *you* love me, my dear?'

Now the youngest daughter didn't like this sort of question, and she didn't believe that her sisters really loved their father as much as she did. She tried to laugh it off, so she said:

'I love you as much as fresh meat needs salt.'

'That means you don't love me at all, you ungrateful thing!' says he, working himself to a passion. 'In my house you shall stay no more!'

The end of it was that nothing she could say would persuade him of the truth, which was that she did love him the best, and he shut his door on her so that all she had got to go out into the wide world with were three dresses.

However, there was nothing for it, away she had to go. On and on she went, till she came to a watery, squelchy bog. And there she gathered

a lot of rushes, and she plaited them up till she made a kind of a cloak with a hood to it and, when she put it on, the cloak covered her from head to foot. After that she went up on to higher ground and hid her three fine dresses under the dry roots of a tree. Then on she went again till at last she came to a great house.

'Do you want a maid?' says she.

'No, we don't,' says they.

'I haven't got anywhere to go,' says she, 'and I'd ask no wages, and do any sort of work.'

'Well,' says they, 'if you like to wash the pots and scrape the saucepans, you can stay.'

So she stayed, and she washed the pots and scraped the saucepans, and did all the dirty work. And because she didn't tell them any name, they called her Cap o' Rushes.

One day there was to be a great dance a little way off, and the servants where she worked were allowed to go and look at the grand people. But Cap o' Rushes said she was too tired to go, so she stayed at home.

But when all the others were gone, she offed with her cap o' rushes and she washed herself in the clear water of the brook, and she went back to the fen and put on a silver dress and went to the ball. And of all the fine folk who were dancing there, there was none so fair or so finely dressed as she.

Who should be at the ball, but her master's son. And what should he do but fall in love with her the moment he set eyes on her. He wouldn't dance with anyone else.

But before the dance was done, Cap o' Rushes slipped off and away she went home. When the other maids got back she was pretending to be asleep with her cap o' rushes on.

Next morning, they said to her:

'You did miss a night, Cap o' Rushes!'

'What was that?' says she.

'Why, the beautifullest lady you ever did see, dressed right gay and gallant. The young master, he never took his eyes off her.'

'Well, I should like to have seen her,' says Cap o' Rushes.

'There's to be another dance this evening, and perhaps she'll be there.'

But come the evening, Cap o' Rushes again said she was too tired to go with them. However, when they were gone, she offed with her cap o' rushes, washed herself in the brook, went back to the fen, and this time the dress she put on was one made all of gold.

The master's son had been reckoning on seeing her, and again he danced with no one else, and never took his eyes off her.

But before the dance was over, she slipped off.

Home she went once more, and, when the maids came back, she pretended to be asleep with her cap o' rushes on.

Next day they said to her again:

'Well, Cap o' Rushes, you should have been there to see the lady. There she was again, right gay and gallant. As for the young master, he never took his eyes off her.'

'Deary me,' says she. 'I should like to have seen her!'

'Well,' says they, 'there's a dance again this evening, and you must go with us, for she's sure to be there.'

Well, come the evening, Cap o' Rushes said for the third time that she was too tired to go, and do what the other servants would to persuade her, she said she would stay at home. But when they were all gone, for the third time she offed with her cap o' rushes, and bathed herself in the brook, went back to the tree, and this time put on a dress that was made of the feathers that had fallen from all the birds that fly in the air. And then, once more, away she went to the dance.

The master's son was overjoyed when he saw her. He danced with none other but her, and never took his eyes off her. But she wouldn't tell him her name, nor where she came from, but at last he gave her a ring, and told her if he didn't see her again he should die.

The dance wasn't over when she slipped away just as before. Home she went, and, for the third time, when the maids came back she was pretending to be asleep with her cap o' rushes on.

Next day they said to her:

'There, Cap o' Rushes! You didn't come last night, and now you won't see the lady, for there's to be no more dances.'

'Well, I should rarely like to have seen her,' says she.

The master's son tried every way to find out where the lady was gone, but go where he might, and ask whom he might, he never heard a thing about her. The end of it was he got paler and paler, and at last he had to keep to his bed he was so ill and all for the love of her.

'Make some gruel for the young master,' they said to the cook. 'He's very sick and near dying for love of the lady.'

The cook had only just set about making the gruel when Cap o' Rushes came in.

'What are you doing?' asks she.

'I'm going to make some gruel for the young master,' says the cook, 'for it seems that he's near dying for love of the lady.'

'Let me make it,' says Cap o' Rushes.

Well the cook wouldn't at first, but at last she agreed; and so it was Cap o' Rushes that made the gruel. When she had made it, she slipped the ring into it on the sly, before the cook took it upstairs.

The young man drank it, and then he saw the ring at the bottom.

'Send for the cook,' says he. So up she comes again.

'Who made this gruel?' says he.

'I did,' said the cook, for she was frightened, you see, but he just looked at her.

'No, you didn't,' says he. 'Say who did, and you shan't be harmed.'

'Well, then, 'twas Cap o' Rushes,' says she.

'Send Cap o' Rushes here,' says he. So Cap o' Rushes came up.

'Did you make the gruel?' says he.

'Yes, I did,' says she.

'Where did you get this ring?' says he.

'From him that gave it me,' says she.

'Who are you, then?' says the young man.

'I'll show you,' says she. And she offed with her cap o' rushes, and there she was in her beautiful clothes, and her lovely long hair hung to her waist.

The master's son he got well very soon, and they were to be married in a little time. It was to be a very grand wedding, and everyone was asked from far and near. Cap o' Rushes' father was one of those that was asked. But nobody knew that he was the bride's father, for still she wouldn't tell anybody who she was.

But before the wedding she went to the kitchen.

'I want you to dress every dish of meat without putting a mite o' salt on it,' says she.

'That'll be rare and nasty,' says the cook.

'Never you mind for that,' says she.

Well, the wedding-day came, and they were married. And after they were married, all the grand company sat down to the wedding feast.

But when they began on the meat, it was so tasteless they couldn't eat it. Cap o' Rushes father, he tried first one dish and then another, and then, what did he do but burst out crying.

'What's the matter?' said the master's son to him.

'Oh,' says he, 'I had a daughter, and I asked her how much she loved me! And she said, 'As much as fresh meat needs salt.' And I turned her away from my door, for I thought she meant she didn't love me. But now, I see that she meant she loved me best of all. And she may be dead now for aught I know.'

'No, father, here she is!' says Cap o' Rushes.

And with that she started up from her place and she ran to him and put her arms round his neck.

And so they all lived happily ever after.

*This tale is found in many countries. This version comes from Suffolk, England.*

# The Great White Cat

ONCE UPON A TIME, far away in the north of Norway, there was a hunter and he caught a big white bear, alive, in a trap. It was such a fine young bear that he hadn't the heart to kill it, so he thought he would take it to the King of Denmark for a present. So he tamed it, and a very good bear it was.

Now, as bear and man plodded along on their long, long journey to the court of the King of Denmark, they came, just on Christmas Eve, to the Dovrafell. Now the Dovrafell is a bad sort of a place at any time of the year. It's a wild moor, all bog and heather and rock, with hardly a tree for shelter, and it's worst of all in the dark of winter, with the wind roaring and a sky full of snow. However, they hadn't gone far when the hunter thought he saw a light. As he got nearer he saw it must be a candle in a cottage window. Very glad he was to see it, in a wild place like that with the snow coming on.

The hunter knocked at the door and greeted the man of the house politely, and asked if he could get house-room there for his bear and himself.

'You might come and welcome,' said the man, whose name was Halvor. 'But deary me! We can't give anyone house-room, not just now!'

'But it's perishing cold out here in the Dovrafell,' said the hunter.

'So it is,' said Halvor, 'and I'm sorry for you, but we have a bad time in this house at this time of the year. Every Christmas, for years now, such a pack of Trolls come down upon us that we are always forced to flit out of the house ourselves! Deary me! These seven years we haven't had so much as a house over our own heads – not at Christmas – and often not a morsel of food. It's very hard on the poor children, so it is!'

'Oh,' said the hunter, 'if that's all, you can very well let in me and my bear. We're not afraid of Trolls. My bear's a quiet fellow. He can lie under the stove yonder, and I can sleep in that little side-room you have by the kitchen.'

Well, at first, Halvor said it would never do, but it was growing so cold outside, and the hunter begged so hard, that, at last, he and his bear were allowed to stay. So in they came. The bear lay down, and the hunter sat by the stove while the woman of the house began to get ready their Christmas dinner with the three children helping her. The hunter thought it was a queer sight to watch them getting the good things ready, for they had never a smile on their faces though they had managed to get together quite a nice feast, so that the hunter's mouth watered. But neither the good woman nor the children nor Halvor were very cheerful about it all, for, you see, they feared that it would only be the Trolls that would get it after all.

Next day was Christmas Day and, sure enough, no sooner had they all sat down to their Christmas dinner than down came

the whole pack of Trolls. Some
came down the chimney and some
came through the windows. They
all shouted and banged about and made such a
hullabaloo that, in a fright, Halvor, his wife, and the
three children got up from their places without having tasted a bite, and
all ran to the woodshed and shut and locked the door. For you see Trolls
are ill creatures and, if it had come to a fight, Halvor thought that the
whole cottage might have been wrecked and the children hurt.

As for the hunter, he sat still in a corner, and watched to see what
would happen. Some of the Trolls were big and some were little, and all
were black and hairy. Some had long tails, and some had no tails at all,
and some had noses as long as pokers. They all went on shouting and
they put their feet and their tails on the table, threw the food about, and
ate and drank, and messed and
tasted everything. The little,
screaming Trolls were the worst.
They pulled each other's tails,
fought over the food and even
climbed up the curtains and began
throwing such things as jars of jam

17

and pickles, *smash*, off the kitchen
shelves.

At last, one of these little Trolls
caught sight of the great white bear,
which all this time lay quiet and
good under the stove. The little
Troll found a piece of sausage and
he stuck it on a fork.

'Pussy! Pussy! Will you have a
bit of sausage?' he screamed as he
poked the fork hard against the
bear's tender black nose. Then he
laughed and pulled it away again so
that the bear couldn't get the sausage.

Then the great white bear was very angry. Up he
rose and, with a growl like thunder, he came out from
under the stove and, in a moment, he had chased the
whole pack of Trolls out of the house.

So the hunter praised him and patted him and gave
him a big bit of sausage to eat in his place under the
stove. Then he called Halvor and the family to come
out of the woodshed. They were very
surprised to find the Trolls gone,
and they cleared up the mess while the hunter
told them what had happened. Then they all sat down

to eat what was left of their Christmas dinner.

The next day the hunter and the bear thanked Halvor and set out again on their long journey to the court of the King of Denmark.

Next year Halvor was out, just about sunset, in a wood at the edge of

the Dovrafell on the afternoon of Christmas Eve. He was busy cutting all
the wood they would want for the holiday. When he stopped to rest for a
moment, leaning on his axe, he heard a voice that seemed to come from
far away on the other side of the wood.

'Halvor! Halvor!' someone was shouting and calling.

'What do you want?' shouted Halvor. 'Here I am.'

'Have you got your big white cat with you still?' called the voice.

'Yes, that I have!' called back Halvor. 'She's lying at home under the
stove this moment. What's more, she has got seven kittens now, each
bigger and fiercer than she is herself!'

'Then we'll never come to see you again!' bawled out the Troll from
the other side of the wood.

What's more he never did, and so, since that time, the Trolls of the Dovrafell have never eaten their Christmas dinner at Halvor's house again.

*A Norse tale*

# Childe Rowland

ONCE UPON A TIME, long ago, there was a queen in England and she had three bold sons and one fair daughter.

One evening the three Princes and Burd Ellen, their sister, were out playing with their golden ball and, as they played, the youngest son, Childe Rowland, sent the ball up so hard that it flew over the church roof.

Off ran their sister, Burd Ellen, to fetch the ball back again. The three Princes waited, but Burd Ellen neither came nor called. Then they went to find her but, search as they would, call as they would, there was no sign of her nor of the ball, and their hearts grew heavy, for they feared that she must have fallen into some evil enchantment.

So, at last, after they had sought her east, and sought her west, and all in vain, and when the Queen, their mother, could do no more but sit on her golden throne and weep, the eldest brother said that he would go and ask the advice of Merlin, the most famous of all the Enchanters of Britain.

So out he set, and when he got to the Enchanter's cave he told Merlin the whole tale – how they four had been playing with their golden ball and how Childe Rowland, the youngest Prince, had sent it high over the church roof, and how their sister, Burd Ellen, had run round calling out to them that she would fetch it back, and how no one had seen her since that day. Then he asked the Enchanter if he could tell what had become of her. Merlin asked the Prince which way round Burd Ellen had run. And when the Prince had answered, Merlin nodded his head.

'Burd Ellen,' said Merlin, 'has fallen under an enchantment because she went round the church "widdershins", that is, the contrary way to the sun. By my art I know that the King of Elfland has carried her off and that he has taken her to his Dark Tower. Hard will it be to win her back.'

'If it is possible – if it is a thing that mortal man may do,' said the Prince, 'I will try.'

'Possible it is,' replied Merlin, 'but woe to any man that tries unless he is well taught beforehand! Boldness is not all!'

Then the eldest Prince begged Merlin to tell him what he must do and what he must not do. Then, after Merlin had taught him, and after he had repeated his lesson, the eldest Prince said farewell to the Queen and his two brothers and rode off on the road to Elfland.

> *But long they waited, and longer still,*
> *With muckle doubt and pain,*
> *And woe were the hearts of his brethren,*
> *For he came not back again.*

After many days had passed, the second brother said that he would try, and he went to the Enchanter Merlin and asked his help to get his sister back again, just as his brother had done. He was given the very same teaching as to how a mortal man might win her back and off he set to ride to Elfland.

> *But long they waited, and longer still,*
> *With muckle doubt and pain,*
> *And woe were his mother's and brother's hearts,*
> *For he came not back again.*

At last, after many days, Childe Rowland, the youngest Prince, wanted to go, so he went to his mother, the good Queen, to ask her blessing. But at first, she would not let him go, for he was the last of her children and if he were lost, all would be lost.

But he begged so long that at last
the Queen said he might go and since
he was their last hope, she gave him
his father's good sword that never
struck in vain. As she buckled the
sword-belt round his waist, the
Queen said the spell that would give
the sword victory and then, as his
brothers had done, Childe Rowland
rode to Merlin's enchanted cave.

'Once more! And but once more, we come to you!' said Childe Rowland, when he stood before Merlin. 'Tell me how a mortal man may rescue the fair Burd Ellen and my two brothers.'

Merlin taught him as he had taught his brothers:

'My son,' said he, 'there are two things, simple they seem, but hard they are to do. One is something that you must do, and one is something you must not do. The thing you must do is this. After you have entered the Kingdom of Elfland, whoever speaks to you, till you see the fair Burd Ellen, you must out with your sword and you must cut off his head. The other is the thing you must not do. However hungry or thirsty you may be, you must drink no drop, nor eat one bite of food while you are in Elfland. If you do, you will never see Middle Earth again!'

Then Merlin told him how he must set out to find Elfland and the

Dark Tower, and that it was the Elf King himself who must be forced to tell him what had become of his two brothers.

Childe Rowland thanked the Enchanter and rode out on the way that his two brothers had ridden and that Merlin had told him.

He went and he went, till at last he came to where a horseherd was sitting with many horses feeding all round him. Childe Rowland could see by their wildness and their fiery eyes that these must be horses of Elfland.

'Can you tell me,' said Childe Rowland to the horseherd, 'where to find the Dark Tower of the King of Elfland?'

'I cannot tell,' said the horseherd, 'but go on a little farther and you will see a cowherd. Maybe he can tell you.'

Then, without a word more, Childe Rowland drew his father's good sword that never struck in vain and off went the horseherd's head. Childe Rowland went on farther till he came to the cowherd and he asked him the same question.

'I cannot tell,' said the cowherd, 'but go on a little farther and you will come to the hen-wife. She is sure to know.'

Then, once more, Childe Rowland drew the good sword that never struck in vain, and off went the cowherd's head.
At last he came to an old woman in a grey cloak, and he asked her if she knew where the Dark Tower of the King of Elfland might be.

'Go on a little farther,' said the hen-wife, 'till you come to a steep, round hill. You must go round it three times widdershins, and, as you go, you must say:

> *Open door! Open door!*
> *And let me come in.*

The third time the door will open, and you may go in.'

Childe Rowland was just going
to ride on when he remembered
what he had to do. So he out with
the good sword that never struck
in vain, and off went the
hen-wife's head.

On he rode till at last he came to
a round, green hill, and when he
saw that, he jumped off his horse.
There was a narrow door in the
side of it, but it was fast shut.
He went round the green hill on
foot, widdershins, and as he went
he said:

> 'Open door! Open door!
> And let me come in.'

Twice he did this and nothing happened. The door
was still fast. But the third time the door opened and
Childe Rowland went in.

Then the door shut again and Childe Rowland
was alone.

It was not exactly dark. There was a kind of
twilight or gloaming, and he seemed to be in a passage that was only
just wide enough for him to pass. There were neither windows nor lamps
and he could not tell where the soft light came from, unless it were
through the walls and roof, which seemed to be made of transparent

rock. The air was warm, as it always is in Elfland.

He went along softly till he saw, at the end of this passage, two wide, high doors and when he pushed on boldly and opened them, he saw a wonderful and glorious sight.

Before him was a large and high hall, as high as a great church. The pillars were all of gold and silver, and round their tops were wreaths of flowers made of diamonds and emeralds and all manner of precious stones. From the very middle of the high roof there hung, by a chain, a huge lamp made out of what seemed to be a great pearl all hollowed out. In the very middle of the pearl was a huge red carbuncle and this gave light to the whole hall.

Far off, at the end of the room, stood a beautiful couch of silk and gold and there, on the couch, whom should he see sitting but his sister, the fair Burd Ellen, combing her golden hair with a silver comb. When she saw Childe Rowland she stood up and her face was full of fear and sorrow as she spoke to him:

> *'God pity you, poor luckless fool,*
> *What have you here to do?*
> *Hear you this, my youngest brother,*
> *Why didn't you bide at home?*
> *Had you a hundred thousand lives*
> *You couldn't spare any a one.*
>
> *But sit you down; but woe, O, woe,*
> *That ever you were born,*
> *For come the King of Elfland in,*
> *Your fortune is forlorn.'*

But Childe Rowland greeted her kindly and embraced her and told her why he had come. When they had sat down together, Childe Rowland asked for news of their two brothers. She wept as she told him how first one and then the other had reached the Dark Tower, but how, in the end, they had been enchanted by the King of Elfland, and now each lay in a stone coffin as if dead.

After they had talked a little, Childe Rowland began to feel faint and hungry from his long travels, and then, forgetting all about Merlin's warning, he begged his sister to give him a little food. At that Burd Ellen looked at him sadly, and shook her head, but because she was under a spell, she could do no more by way of warning. Instead, she was obliged to rise, and go out and soon she brought back a golden basin full of bread and milk. Childe Rowland was just going to raise it to his lips, when, catching sight of the sad face of his sister, he remembered just in time, and suddenly dashed bowl and all to the ground, saying:

'Not a sup will I swallow, not a bit will I bite, till Burd Ellen is free.'

Just as he spoke they heard the noise of heavy footsteps and soon a loud voice crying:

*'Fee, fi, fo, fum,*
*I smell the blood of a Christian man,*

> *Be he alive or be he dead,*
> *I'll dash his brains from his brain-pan.'*

With that, the great doors of the hall burst open, and in rushed the terrible King of Elfland with his drawn sword flashing in his hand. But Childe Rowland was not afraid, for he stood ready with his sword.

'Strike then, Bogle, if you dare!' he shouted and rushed to meet the Elf King.

They fought. For long they fought. Sometimes one seemed to be winning and sometimes the other, but at last Childe Rowland had beaten the King of Elfland down on to his knees and, as he stood over him with his raised sword, the Elf King begged for mercy.

'I will give you mercy, and spare your life,' said Childe Rowland, 'if you swear to release my sister from your spells. Then you must raise my brothers to life, and, after all that is done, you must let us all go out free from your Dark Tower.'

The beaten Bogle had to agree to this, so Childe Rowland let him get up. Then the Elf King went to a strong chest, and from it he took a little crystal bottle filled with something blood-red. Then Childe Rowland was taken to where his two brothers lay as if dead in their stone coffins.

But now, with his red salve, the Elf King touched their ears, eyelids, nostrils, lips and finger-tips. No sooner had he done this than they sprang up, as well as ever they had been, and told Childe Rowland that their souls had been far away, but had now come back to them. Next the Elf King said

some words over Burd Ellen and the spell was taken off her too. And then he gave the little crystal bottle of salve to Childe Rowland. So, at last, they all passed out of the splendid hall of the defeated Elf King. Through the long passage they went and out of the door, which opened at their touch but shut again behind them. Glad they were to see wholesome daylight again and to turn their backs on the Dark Tower.

Then, as they went on their homeward way rejoicing, Childe Rowland remembered the hen-wife, the cowherd and the horseherd. There they lay, all three, where he had left them, but with a touch of the red salve, Childe Rowland was able to restore them to life.

When at last they all reached home, the good Queen their mother laughed for joy, and she ordered a great feast, so that everyone, great and small, in the whole kingdom, should be able to rejoice with her, because the fair Burd Ellen and her three brothers were safe home again.

*An English tale*

# The King, the Saint and the Goose

DID YOU EVER HEAR what happened to good King O'Toole, who lived long ago in Ireland, and how it was that his old age was made pleasant to him?

If you never heard it, isn't it high time you did?

Now, in his young days, King O'Toole had been one of the finest young fellows in all Ireland. He loved hunting better than anything in the world, and from the rising of the sun till darkness came, he would be out galloping and hallooing with his horse and his hounds.

This went on merrily for a long while, but in the end the King grew too old and too stiff to be hunting all day, summer and winter, be it wet or be it fine. Indeed a winter came when it was as much as the poor old

King could do to hobble about with a stick or even a crutch. Why, then it's lost he was, for he felt as if there wasn't any amusement or diversion

left for him in the world.

So at last, what did that poor old King do, but tame a wild goose to amuse and divert him. You may laugh, but she was a very good, faithful creature was that goose.

For a while they had a lot of pleasure together, her and King O'Toole. She would fly round and about, but would always come back when he called her and would waddle after him if that was what would please him. On a Friday (that, you know, is a fast day) she would swim far out into the lake, two or three times, and come back each time to him with a nice plump trout for his dinner.

So that good creature was

all poor old King O'Toole's amusement and pleasure. But my dear! The sadness of the world! The time came when the poor old goose grew too old too, and one winter the truth was that she was as stiff in the wing as her master was in the leg, so that, try as she would, the poor faithful creature couldn't amuse him any more. Why then, the old King was lost entirely and had no more pleasure in life.

One day these two distressful creatures were sitting by the side of the lake. The King had his poor old goose in his arms, and he was looking down fondly at her, the tears in his eyes, lamenting because neither he nor she had any more pleasure. Then, presently, he let her go and she waddled off to get a bite to eat. But the old King sat on, thinking that he might as well be dead and drowned in the lake, as live such a miserable and distressful life.

Then he happened to look up, and what should he see standing before him but a decent young fellow that seemed to be a stranger to those parts.

'God save you, King O'Toole,' said the decent young fellow.

'How come you know my name?' says the King.

'Never mind for that!' answered the fellow. 'I know a lot of what passes. And may I make bold to ask how is your goose, King O'Toole?'

'And how come you know about my goose?' asked the King (for you see she was out of sight now, among the weeds).

'I know all about her. No matter how,' said the young fellow smiling.

'And who may you be?' asked the King.

'An honest man,' answered the fellow.

'And how do you get a living?' asked the King.

'By making old things as good as new.'

'Is it a tinker you are then?' asked the King.

'No. I've got a better trade than that. What would you say, King O'Toole, if I were to offer to make your goose as good as new?'

'As good as new?' asked the King, and he smiled all over his poor old face, thinking that, of all the pleasures of this world, that would please him the best.

'Yes! As good as new,' said the young fellow nodding.

King O'Toole gave a whistle, and out of the reeds came his poor old goose, waddling and limping. As obedient as a hound she was, that creature, and faithful to her poor old crippled master. When the

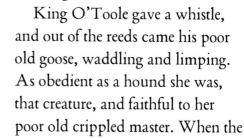

young man looked down and saw her he nodded again.

'Yes,' says he, 'I could do the job for you easy enough.'

'By the holy word,' says the King, looking down in his turn and seeing the poor old bag-of-bones of a goose. 'If you can do that, why you're the cleverest young fellow in seven parishes!'

'I'm better than that, bedad,' says the young man laughing, 'but what will you give me now, if I do the job for you?'

'I'll give you whatever you ask for,' says the King. 'Isn't that fair enough?'

'Will you give me all the ground the goose covers the first time she flies after she's been made as good as new?'

'Indeed I will,' says the King.

'You'll not go back on your word?' says the young fellow.

'I will not,' says the King.

Then the young man called to the poor bag-of-bones of a goose:

'You poor unhappy old cripple!' says he, catching her gently by the wings. 'It's I that will make you a fine sporting bird again!' With that he made the sign of the cross over her and then he threw her up into the air and, as he threw her, he blew at her feathers just to give her a bit of a lift. Sakes alive! If that goose didn't fly off from his hand as if it was one of the eagles of the mountains that she was. Aye, and she sported and capered in the air with delight, just like any swallow.

It was a beautiful sight to see the old King, for he was there with his mouth open for joy and surprise, looking at his poor old goose, and she flying as light as a lark in the sky.

Well, she had a good fly round – out of sight and back again – then she lit down at her master's feet with a shake of her wings. When he had patted her head and stroked her all down her back he could tell that she was as good, and even better, than ever she had been.

'Sure, you're the darling of the world,' says the old King to the goose.

'And what do you say to me?' asked the young fellow.

'I say you're the cleverest fellow that walks the ground of Ireland,' replied the King, still looking at his goose.

'No more than that?'

'I say I'll be grateful to you to my dying day.'

'But will you do as you said and give me the land that the goose flew over just now?'

'I will,' said the King, looking up at last. 'You'd be welcome to it if it was the last acre I'd got.'

'You're a good, decent old man, for you keep to a bargain,' says the young fellow, 'and well for you and your goose that you are, else your bird would never fly again!'

'But who are you?' asked the King for the second time that morning, for he seemed to see a change coming over the young fellow.

'I'm St Kevin,' he answered.

'Oh, Queen of Heaven!' said the King, making the sign of the cross, and dropping to his knees as well as he could for the stiffness of his joints. 'And is it with a holy saint I've been speaking and discoursing all this while?'

'It is,' said St Kevin.

'And me thinking it was only a decent young lad!'

'I came in disguise,' said the saint, 'so how would you be knowing with whom you were talking and discoursing? I came to try you, King O'Toole, and I've been finding this morning that you're a decent old King, for it seems that you'll keep a bargain even with one you took to be no more than a tinker.'

Well, King O'Toole had kept his bargain, so sure enough he had his goose as good as new to amuse and divert him till the day he died, and though 'twas only a little bit of a kingdom that he had left, the saint evermore provided for the two of them — for the King and the goose.

So now you know how it came about that all that queer-shaped bit of ground in that part of Ireland belongs to one of the saints of Heaven.

*An Irish tale*

# The Country of
# The Mice

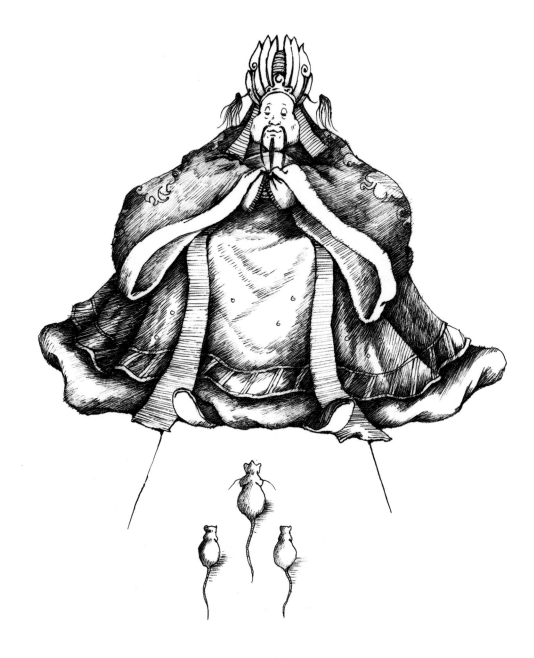

THERE WAS ONCE a part of Tibet where there were two strange laws. The first of these was that no-one, on pain of death, might keep a cat. The second was that in a certain valley – down which ran a big mountain stream – the monks of the nearby monastery must keep the stone embankment on their side in good repair. These two laws were made for a very special reason and if you read on you will know what that reason was.

The man who was, long ago, the King of this part of Tibet, was an excellent man. One day, as he was sitting on his throne in the inner courtyard of his palace, he was told that a very grandly dressed mouse, with a number of attendant mice, was at the gate, and that the grand mouse was asking to see him.

The King was very much amused at the idea of having a visit from a talking mouse and he gave orders that this splendid fellow, and his attendants, were to be brought in at once.

Now it is the custom in Tibet for all visitors – at any rate on great occasions – to bring with them a present of a white silk scarf. The King was delighted to see that, when he came before the throne, the mouse knew all about this custom, and that he brought, not exactly a scarf, but a beautiful single thread of white silk. The silk thread was handed by one of the mouse's attendants to one of the King's guards, with a low bow.

The King now politely bade the mouse welcome and soon the visitor was explaining why he had come.

'O King,' began the mouse, 'you must know that this year our harvest was bad, our crops have fallen short, and we are threatened with hunger and famine unless we can borrow enough grain to carry us through the winter. So I, who am ruler and chief of all the mice of your country, stand before you here to ask if you can help us. If you can lend us what barley and oats we need, we will not only pay you back faithfully at our next harvest, but, as interest, with more grain than you lend us.'

'Very well,' agreed the King. 'We will lend. How much do you want?'

'I think,' said the mouse, 'that we shall need about one of your big barns full.'

'Good gracious!' said the King, astonished. 'And if I really do lend you a whole barnful of grain, how in the world do you think you could ever carry it away?'

'Leave that to me!' replied the mouse in a confident tone. 'If you will consent to lend the grain, we will do the rest.'

So the King agreed to lend the mice one of his great granaries full of barley and oats. He decided on the largest and ordered his officers to throw open its doors, and to let the mice carry away as much as they wanted.

That night, the chief and ruler of the mice summoned his subjects together, and, to the number of many hundreds of thousands, they came to the barn. Then each mouse picked up as much grain as he could carry. One mouse would hold it in his mouth, another in a tiny sack on his back, and others had some curious way of carrying it curled up in their tails. They made a very tidy job of it and when they had finished, the barn was completely empty, and not a single grain of barley or oats was left behind.

Next morning, when the King went out to look at his barn, he was very much astonished to find that the mice really had been able to take the grain away so quickly, and he began to have a very high opinion of them.

'These are very efficient mice,' said he to his courtiers.

When, after the next harvest, the chief and ruler of the mice kept his

promise and paid back the grain with interest, the King decided that the mice were honest as well as clever.

Now it happened, not long after this, that the country over which this King ruled was attacked by the ruler of a neighbouring kingdom. This kingdom lay on the opposite side of the big mountain and river, and was far richer and more powerful than the country where the mice lived. Soon a large army was on the march and ready to attack.

When the mice heard what was happening they were very worried, for they feared that, if the enemy entered their country and dethroned the King who had been their friend over the loan of the grain, they themselves might not be so well off. In fact, they did not like the idea of a strange ruler.

So the mouse put on his grandest robes, and, with his attendants, set out to visit the King again. When he got to the palace he again asked for an interview with his majesty. He was shown in at once, and once more offered a single thread instead of the usual scarf. Finding that the King was looking very depressed, the mouse chief spoke at once in a grand but squeaky manner:

'I have come to you a second time, O King, in order to see whether I can be of use to you. The last time I was here you did me and my people a great favour, and if it is now in our power to help in any way, we shall be very glad to do our best.'

In spite of feeling depressed about the war, the King could not but feel amused to hear such solemn words from a mouse.

'I thank you very much,' said he, 'but really what could your excellent mice do to help? We are threatened with invasion by a foreign army, outnumbering mine by many thousands. This army is already encamped just across the river. All the men I can muster will not be enough to prevent them from crossing as soon as they choose. Thank you yet again, but I don't see how mice could help.'

'Do you remember, O King,' replied the mouse in a calm tone, 'that on the first occasion I was here you did not believe that we should be able to carry away the grain you had lent us, or to pay back the loan? And yet we proved ourselves able to do both! All we ask you now is to trust us again, and, if you will undertake to do one or two things which we will ask of you, we, on our part, will undertake to rid you of the invading army.'

The King was very interested, and he replied:

'Very well, mouse. What you say is true. I didn't believe last time you would be able to do what you said but I trusted you and I will trust you again. Tell me now what you wish my servants or my army to do, and I will see that they carry out our share of the bargain.'

'Very good,' answered the mouse. 'All we wish you to do is provide us, by tomorrow evening, with one hundred thousand sticks. Each stick must be about a foot long, and they must all be laid neatly in rows on the bank of the river. If you will undertake to do this, we on our side will undertake to put the opposing army in a state of confusion and panic! But I should like to add something more. If we succeed in doing all we promise, we shall, later, ask you to safeguard us against the two

principal dangers which threaten our existence.'

'If you can really do what you say,' replied the King, 'I will certainly try to safeguard you against these dangers, if you tell me what they are.'

'The dangers to which I refer,' answered the mouse, 'are, gracious King, the dangers of floods and cats. Most of our mouse-holes – our homes – are in the low-lying land near the river, and whenever the snows melt and the river rises, it overflows this level country and floods our holes and nests. What we would suggest to your majesty, is that you should build a strong wall – an embankment – all along the river, so as to make sure that the water cannot overflow into our homes. As to cats, they are always the persecutors of mice, and we ask you to banish all cats for ever from your kingdom.'

'Very well,' replied the King, 'if you succeed in getting rid of the large and powerful army which now threatens us, I will undertake to do what you ask.'

On hearing this the mouse chief bowed low to the King, and, after making polite farewells, he went back as fast as he could to his own subjects.

Next morning, early, he sent out messengers to call together all the

full-grown mice of his kingdom, and, when they came, he gave them his orders. About dusk he was able to lead a large army, numbering several hundreds of thousands of mice, to the bank of the river, where he found the sticks all neatly laid out exactly as the King had promised.

The mice had fully understood the orders they had been given, and each small group at once proceeded to launch a stick on the river, by means of which they soon crossed over to the other side.

It was quite dark by the time they got across and the enemy soldiers were all asleep in their camp. Some were lying in tents and some were lying outside in blankets, but all had their weapons beside them ready for any alarm. But no alarm was given. The mice were sound-less. They did not even need a word of command from their chief, but at once scattered themselves through the camp, whereupon each one began to do as much damage as he

possibly could in the shortest possible time.

Some went to the bowmen and nibbled their bow-strings. Some went to where the musketeers were sleeping and gnawed through their musket-slings. Others bit holes in the clothes of the men and some bit off their pigtails. Others bit holes in sacks so that everything in them spilled.

In fact, these bold mice attacked anything upon
which their teeth could make an impression, so that
tents, stores, grain, and provisions of all kinds were
soon in shreds or scattered in confusion.

After a couple of hours of such silent work the chief
collected his mouse army on the river bank, and,
embarked on their stick-rafts once more, they paddled
themselves quietly over to their own shore without
a sound having been heard by
the enemy.

But next morning, at day break,
when the enemy soldiers began to
stir, there was a fearful outcry in the
camp. Each man as he woke from
sleep found himself in a woeful state
– his clothes in rags, his pigtail
nibbled, his bow-string gnawed, his
musket without a sling to carry it or
a fuse to light it. What was almost
worse – there was nothing to eat for
breakfast! No – not a single crumb!
Each soldier at once began to accuse
the other of theft and treachery.
Before many minutes had passed
the whole camp was in uproar,
comrade quarrelling with comrade,
and every man in the field was
accusing the other.

The mouse ruler had, of course,
advised the King that now was the
time for the King's small army to
attack. He did not actually do more
than march down to the river, but

he flew the great flag in the blue sky
and had the great drum beaten on
the terrace of the palace. So, in the
middle of their confusion, the enemy soldiers on the
opposite bank saw the flag and heard the great drum
and, terrified at the thought of having to fight in their
present confusion, the whole enemy army took flight.

As for the mice, safe from floods and cats, they
lived happily, and every year the King also provided for them a gift of
grain in thankful recognition of the splendid help they had given him in
time of need.

The King naturally wanted to make quite sure that there would not
be any more invasions. What he did, after thanking the mice, was to
send a herald across the river to the enemy capital. The herald was told to
say that, on this occasion, the King had only considered it worthwhile to
employ a few mice to defeat his enemies. But if he was ever threatened
again, he would be ready to beat back the attack first with all his cows,
sheep, yaks, cats and dogs; and if they did not succeed, he would order
out mountain tigers, wild dogs, wolves and bears, and if they failed, he
would come out to war himself with all his warriors!

When the foreign ruler heard this message he was very frightened and
considered it wiser at once to make a treaty of peace.

'How,' he said to himself, 'can I hope to defeat even

the tame animals, let alone the wild beasts and the soldiers, of a country whose mice can show such skill and courage?'

So peace was made and the two countries remained on friendly terms for many years after.

*A Tibetan tale*

# The Well of
# the World's End

LONG AGO, in a lonely cottage, a girl lived
with her mother who was a widow woman. One
day the widow gave her a sieve and told her to go and fill it with water
from the Well of the World's End. 'And,' said she, 'mind you bring it
home to me full.'

At that the girl was very sad, and taking the sieve she started off with a
heavy heart. As she went she asked everyone she met where the Well of
the World's End might be. But nobody knew, and she couldn't tell
what to do. However, she went, and she went, and at last she met a queer
old woman, all bent double, and the girl asked her too.

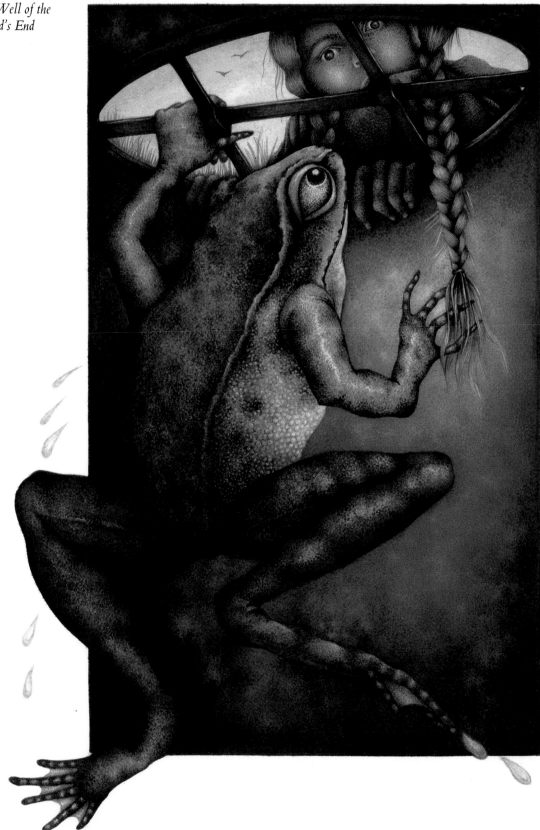

'Can you tell me, please,' said she, 'where is the Well of the World's End?'

The old woman answered her kindly and told her just where to find it, and how she was to go to get to it. So the girl thanked her, did just as the old woman said and, sure enough, she did find the well.

But dear, dear, her troubles were not ended yet for, as you can guess, when the girl dipped the sieve into the cold, cold well the water all ran out again. The girl tried and she tried, but it was no use, so at last she sat down on the edge of the well and she cried as if her heart would break.

Suddenly she heard a strange croaking voice:

'What is the matter, my dear?' said the voice, and with that she looked up. There sat a great frog, with large round eyes, looking at her.

'Matter enough!' said the girl still crying, and then she told the frog how hard it had been to find the well and what her mother had said, and how, every time she dipped the sieve in the well, all the water ran out.

'If you promise,' said the frog, 'to do whatever I tell you for a whole night long, I'll help you. I'll tell you how to fill your sieve with the water from the Well of the World's End.'

The girl thought the frog seemed friendly enough.

'And what harm can a frog do me anyhow?' she thought. So she agreed, and then the frog said in its strange croaking voice:

> *'Stuff it with moss and daub it with clay*
> *And then it will carry the water away.'*

No sooner had it said the last word than it gave a jump, and *plop*, *splash*, it disappeared into the cold, dark water of the Well of the World's End.

So the girl did just as the frog had told her. She found some moss and stuffed it between the holes in the sieve, and then she found some clay and she daubed it on the moss very carefully. Then she let it all dry a bit in the sun, and at last, once more, she dipped the sieve into the cold, cold waters of the well. This time the water did not run out and, with a light heart, the girl started off home. As she went she turned to have a last look at the Well of the World's End and, as she looked, the frog popped his head out of the well and he said:

'Remember your promise.' The girl nodded.

'All right,' she said, and she thought again, 'what harm can a frog do me?'

So back she went and, this time, the way didn't seem long at all and she brought the sieve full of water to her mother.

That very evening, as the two of them sat by the fire, they heard something tapping at the door, low down, and a voice said:

> *'Open the door, my honey, my heart,*
> *Open the door, my own darling;*
> *Mind you the words that you and I spoke,*
> *Down at the World's End Well.'*

As you can guess, the mother was surprised to hear that. But the girl knew well enough who was at the door, and so she told her mother all about it.

'You must keep your promise, girl,' said the mother. 'Go and open the door.'

So the girl got up, and she opened the door, and, sure enough, there was the great frog on the doorstep, and it was so wet that the water ran off the stone and down the path. It gave a hop right into the room and right up to the girl's feet, and when she took a step back to her chair, it took another big hop after her. It looked up at her with its great round eyes and said:

> *'Lift me to your knee, my honey, my heart,*
> *Lift me to your knee, my own darling;*
> *Remember the words that you and I spoke,*
> *Down by the World's End Well.'*

As you can guess, the girl didn't much like the idea of that, for, as you know, the frog was dripping wet. But her mother said:

'Girls must keep their promises.' At that the girl sat by the fire again
and she lifted the frog on to her lap, and it was so wet that her apron and
her dress were both soaked through in a moment, and it was so cold that
it seemed to the girl as if the fire gave no heat.

For a long while the frog said never a word, but at last it spoke again:

> *'Give me some supper, my honey, my heart,*
> *Give me some supper, my darling;*
> *Remember the words that you and I spoke,*
> *Down by the World's End Well.'*

The girl was glad enough to do that, so she got up and sat the frog on the
chair, but the frog was so wet the water ran down to the floor. The girl
made ready a bowl of bread and milk, and she fed the
frog with a spoon, and when it had finished, it said:

> *'Go with me to bed, my honey, my heart,*
> *Go with me to bed, my own darling;*
> *Mind you the words you spoke to me,*
> *Down by the cold well, so weary.'*

Well, the girl did not want to do
that. She did not want to take the
cold wet frog into her bed, but her
mother said again:

'Girls must keep their promises.'
So sadly and sorrowfully, the girl
took the frog with her to bed and, as
you can guess, she kept it as far
away from her as she could, and it is
little sleep she got that night. Well,
just as dawn was breaking she heard
the frog speaking again, and this is
what it said:

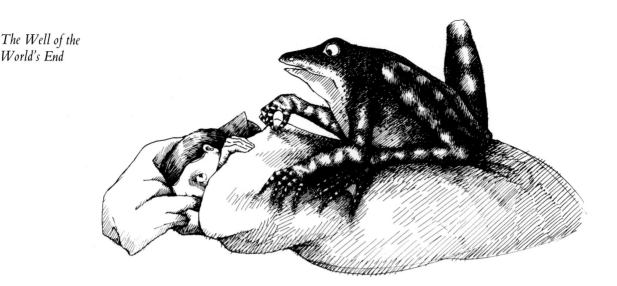

> *'Chop off my head, my honey, my heart,*
> *Chop off my head, my own darling;*
> *Remember the promise you made to me,*
> *Down by the cold well, so weary.'*

Well, the girl was very sorry to hear the frog say that, for she remembered how it had been kind to her and how it had taught her to fill the sieve with water and, wet and cold though it was, she thought now that it was quite a pretty creature.

But the frog said again in its queer croaking voice:

> *'Chop off my head, my honey, my heart,*
> *Chop off my head, my own darling;*
> *Remember the promise you made to me,*
> *Down by the cold well, so weary.'*

When she still didn't want to do it, the frog repeated the words a third time. So the girl saw there was no help for it. She went and found the axe, and she put the frog on the floor, and with tears running from her eyes she chopped off its head.

Then what do you think happened? There in front of her, instead of the frog, there stood a handsome young prince, and he didn't speak with a frog's croaking voice any more, but with his own clear voice. He took the girl by the hand and he told her that he had been enchanted by a wicked witch and that, now, the girl had broken the spell for him, for the spell was that in his frog state, he had to find a girl who would do his bidding for a whole night.

So they were married and they went to live in the castle of the King, his father. There was great rejoicing because now the spell was off, and he was a prince again, and they lived happily ever after.

*An English tale*

# The Magic Bird

*Hear my tale! What happened did not happen in my village,*
*nor did it happen in your village.*
*All the same it was in Africa that it happened.*

THE TRIBE that lived in this village didn't have any cattle. No! They grew kaffir-corn and ground-nuts and maize and such crops as that in their gardens and fields. Now and then they traded the things they could grow with the people of other tribes who kept cows. Unless they did this they never had a chance to taste milk, or curds-and-whey, or butter, or cream, though they liked these things just as much as you do, and as I do. Sometimes they managed to grow very good crops in their clearings, but that didn't always happen and, as I've told you, there were no cows at all. No cows!

One year the crops were really bad, so all the people of the tribe thought that they would try fresh ground and go hoeing and sowing in a place that had never been gardened before. So that's what they did, they all went off to work on new ground.

One of the men who went was called Masilo. His wife and their two children, who were called Duma and Dumasine – a boy and a girl – went with him. The first thing that Masilo did when they got to the new garden-strip was to make a little branch shelter, a sort of small green hut to rest in for an hour at noon in the great heat, and then, for the rest of the day, he and his wife and the two children worked at clearing the ground of weeds and stones. After that they hoed it, ready to put in the seed.

That evening, when the sun began to get low and it was time for everyone to go back to the village, Masilo and his wife and children went back with the rest. They all walked along the path with their hoes over their shoulders.

But then, what do you think? As soon as everyone was out of sight, a beautiful bird flew down and came and sat on the roof of the little shelter that Masilo had built, and as soon as it had perched it began to whistle and sing. The tune was nice enough, but oh dear! What sort of words did that pretty bird sing?

> *'Chanchassa Chanchassa Kilhiso!*
> *Ground, put yourself back!*
> *Be as you were,*
> *Strip that was hoed by Masilo!'*

Could you believe it, my children? That was exactly what the strip did. All the weeds that had been there blew back or rolled back, and took root again, and all the grass-sods and the stones that they had worked so hard to hoe up, all put themselves back as well. The other people's garden-strips were all right, but it didn't look as if anyone had worked on poor Masilo's strip at all.

Next morning, when Masilo and his wife and children came back with the seed they couldn't believe their eyes.

'Can that really be the garden-strip that we all cleared and hoed so nicely yesterday?' they asked each other. 'The strip that was all tidy and ready for sowing?' But though they were terribly disappointed they could

see that it really was the same strip, because, you see, to the right and left of it, the very same neighbours who had worked alongside of them the day before were busy once more. Both lots of neighbours had brought their seeds, so now they could begin sowing because their strips were all right.

When the others looked up from their work and saw Masilo's ground they laughed:

'You really are a lazy lot, Masilo! You and your family are bone-idle – that's what's wrong!'

Well, Masilo and his wife were too miserable to answer back and thought that there was nothing for it but to try again. The sun was very hot but, in spite of that, they and the children worked all day and, by evening, they had once more got the whole strip ready for sowing. So, at last, very tired, off they all four went, home with the others.

But it was all no good! No sooner were they out of sight than the beautiful bird came back.

What a bird it was! Its wings were scarlet, its long tail was steely blue, it had patches of white that shone like silver on its back, and its pretty round head shone like gold. Once more it flew down to the top of Masilo's little shelter-hut, once more it began to whistle and sing. The tune was very pretty, but I am sorry to tell you, oh my children, the words were the same that it had sung before:

'*Chanchassa Chanchassa Kilhiso!*
*Ground, put yourself back!*

*Be as you were,*
*Strip that was hoed by Masilo!'*

And when the beautiful bird had done singing, that strip was as bad as ever again, and once more it looked as if no-one had ever worked on it.

When Masilo and his wife and the two children came back next morning, they really were most bitterly disappointed. But what could they do? Again, all day, they worked in the hot sun. But then, something different happened. In the evening, when the sun was ready to set, Masilo said:

'Someone or something has bewitched this strip. Go home, wife, and take the children with you, and I'll stay here and see what sort of creature it can be that has spoilt all our work.'

So his wife and the two children, Duma the boy, and Dumasine the girl, joined the long line of tired people who were all winding back along the narrow path to the village. But Masilo didn't go. He hid under the little branch shelter that he had built.

He hadn't long to wait. Soon he saw a most beautiful bird which flew down and perched itself on the roof of the shelter, just above the place where he was hidden. Such a beautiful bird Masilo had never seen. Its red and steely blue and silver shone in the setting sun and so did its golden head and, what's more, it seemed to be a most gay and cheerful bird. It hopped about, it flapped its scarlet wings, it spread its steel-blue tail, and then it began to whistle. The tune was pretty enough! But as soon as it began to sing, the third day's work was spoiled.

*'Chanchassa Chanchassa Kilhiso!*
*Ground, put yourself back!*
*Be as you were,*
*Strip that was hoed by Masilo!'*

Then Masilo, who was crouching just below it, hidden in the shelter, stretched up his hand through the loose branches and caught the bird by the legs. The creature flapped its scarlet wings and struggled and tried to get away, but Masilo held on tight.

'So it's YOU, you cruel bird, that's spoilt all our work! All the work that we'd done in the hot sun,' cried Masilo. Then, still holding the bird's legs with one hand, he took out his big sheath-knife and got ready to cut its head off.

'Don't kill me!' said the bird. 'I'll make you as much milk and curds and cream as ever you like!'

'YOU make milk and curds and cream? But you're a bird!' said Masilo.

'You'll soon see!' said the bird.

'I don't believe a word of it!' answered Masilo and then he hesitated. 'But anyhow, before I really decide not to cut your head off, I shall have to have some sort of proof that you're really able to work good magic as well as bad.'

'Watch this then!' said the bird, and it sang these words but to another tune:

*'Chanchassa Chanchassa Kilhiso!*
*Get yourself ready for sowing,*
*Ground that was hoed by Masilo!'*

Would you believe it! In a minute, the strip was all ready for sowing again. There wasn't a weed or stone on it.

Then Masilo, still holding on to the bird with one hand, put away the sheath-knife and then picked a big leaf with the other hand and said:

'Now let's see if you can do what you boasted about! Let's see if you can fill this leaf with milk or with curds-and-whey.'

Do you know, oh my children, that that's just what the bird did? It clapped its wings two or three times so quickly that Masilo couldn't see exactly what it was doing. But what he did see was that the big leaf was soon full of delicious curds-and-whey. Masilo was hungry and thirsty and so, in case it all disappeared again, he swallowed it all up at once.

So then he pulled an old sack out of the shelter and then started to carry the bird off to his hut. But he didn't want anyone to see what he'd got, so, before he came to the village, he put the bird in the sack.

When he was safe inside his house he carefully shut all the openings and said to his wife:

'Wife! Wash out all the biggest pots that we've got, the ones that we brew beer in!'

'What's the sense of doing that?' asked his wife. 'We've got nothing to put in them!'

'Just you listen to me!' answered Masilo. 'Just do what I ask you! Then you'll see!'

So the wife did as her husband asked, and she cleaned out all the big beer crocks and pots. Then Masilo told the two children to go outside and, when they'd gone, he pulled the bird out of the sack.

'Now, you bird you! Fill all those crocks and pots with milk or curds or cream! Don't forget that you spoilt three days' work on our strip, so give us plenty or it'll be the worse for you.'

The bird began to spread its wings and tail and dance about and clap its wings and, sure enough, in another moment, all those big pots and crocks were full either of delicious milk or curds or cream.

When all this was done, Masilo put the bird back in the sack, hid it, and called the children. Then they all sat down and had the best meal they'd had for a long time.

'Now remember,' said Masilo to his children, Duma and Dumasine, 'don't you tell anybody what sort of a supper you had tonight! Be sure not to tell the other children.'

No indeed, they said, they'd never tell a word.

This went on for a long time. They always had a good supper when they got back tired from the garden-strip, so Masilo and his wife and the two children got so fat and sleek that people were surprised to see how plump and well they looked.

'Why,' they said, 'is everybody in Masilo's house so fat? He has always been very poor. But now, already, since he made that new garden, though the crops aren't ripe enough to eat yet, all the same he and his wife and the two children are so fat you could roll them down the hill!'

The neighbours tried their best to look into Masilo's hut because they hoped to see what it was they were getting to eat, but in vain.

Then, one morning, Masilo and his wife went with the others to work in their gardens as usual. This time, however, the children didn't go with them. All the children in the village went out to play instead.

The others said to Masilo's children:

'Oh Duma and Dumasine! Tell us how it is that while we're so thin, you're so fat?'

'Are we fat?' asked Duma and Dumasine. 'We thought we were just as thin as you are!'

The two children answered like that, you see, because they didn't want to say anything about *why* it was that they had such sleek, shiny,

black skins. But the other children weren't going to be content with
nonsense like that.

'Of course you're fatter than we are!' they said. 'Oh, do, oh do
tell us the secret! We won't tell anyone else! We won't tell any of the
grown-ups.'

'All right,' said Duma and Dumasine at last. 'We'll tell you! In our
father's house there's a bird that makes milk. It makes milk come into all
the pots and crocks that we used to use for making beer and we get curds
and cream as well as milk.'

But of course the other children wouldn't believe them.

'How could a bird make milk come?' they said.

'We'll show you!' said Duma and Dumasine at last.

So into the hut they all went, and Masilo's two children pulled the
bird out of the secret place where their father had hidden it. Then they
did just as they had seen their father do, and soon the beautiful bird, with
a cord round one leg, stood in the middle of the hut tied to a big stool. It
danced about and waved and clapped its scarlet wings and spread its
steel-blue tail and, in a moment, all the pots and all the crocks in the hut
were full of milk and cream and curds.

'Help yourselves!' cried Duma and Dumasine proudly. Soon all the
children were having a splendid time feasting, for they were all hungry,
every one of them, and they knew that at home there wouldn't be much
supper – not till the next crops were ready.

After they had feasted they all admired and stroked the beautiful bird.
At last one of the children said:

'I believe that this bird could dance even better if we untied it.
It doesn't like the cord – but just look at its lovely feathers!'

So the children did untie it and it danced in the middle of the hut
while all the children clapped in time to its dancing. After a while the
bird said:

'There isn't really room to dance properly here. Why not take me
outside?'

So the children carried the bird outside and they all stood round it
laughing and singing and dancing, while the bird danced in the middle,

bending its golden head, spreading its steel‑blue tail and flapping its beautiful scarlet wings.

But oh my children! Can you guess what happened? I expect you can! After quite a short time the bird flew right out of the circle of children and perched high on a tree‑top, well out of reach, and there it sat, as cheerful as could be, whistling its tune. Goodness, weren't the children frightened then! Masilo's boy and girl, Duma and Dumasine, were the most frightened of all and the girl cried:

'We *must* try and catch it! Our father will be very, very angry!'

So the whole lot of children set off after it. And do you know what the bird did? It led them on.

First it would fly for a short way, then it would hop and flutter

as if it couldn't fly any more and then it would stand quite still. But as soon as a child got near enough to pounce, off it flew again.

Well, after a while the neighbours' children had had enough of it and went home, but Masilo's children – Duma and Dumasine – decided they must keep trying to get the bird back. So they kept on going a little farther and a little farther, always hoping that, next time, the bird would really stop and that they would be able to catch it.

At last evening came, and Masilo and his wife came back from their garden-strip. But their hut was empty, there was no bird there, and no children. So they wondered what had happened. They minded most about the bird for they thought the children were still out playing, so at first they didn't bother much about them but just felt sad and rather angry about the bird, and didn't know how they were ever going to have any more of the delicious cream and curds-and-whey. When evening came they began to get anxious about the children as well. They called and called. But no-one seemed to know anything, because the neighbours' children, who knew quite a lot, never said a word.

As for Duma and Dumasine, when it began to get dark they thought they had better go back to

their parents even though they hadn't been able to catch the bird.

So what happened then? What happened then, oh my children, was a terrible storm with rain and thunder. It gradually got worse and huge hailstones, big! big as pigeons' eggs, began to fall, so the two children sheltered under a big tree. The storm went on for a long time – all night – but at last with the first light it cleared and then Duma and Dumasine came out and, as they came out, they looked up at the tree.

They saw that this tree was covered with beautiful black fruits – rather like small black plums those fruits were – and they didn't seem to have been bruised by the storm. The children, who were very hungry by this time, each picked and ate a few that grew low enough to reach. And what do you think happened then? All the other plums, that were still growing on the tree, turned into little tiny birds that twittered and flew about. Then, in the middle of this cloud of tiny birds, they spied the magic bird.

Bright as a flower he was, and as cheerful as ever, spreading his scarlet wings, wagging his steel-blue tail up and down, whistling and dancing. The children hated the sight of him. At last the bird spoke:

'I suppose I'd better do something for you two children,' said he. 'After all, it was you who set me free!' So he bowed his beautiful golden head and snapped two little twigs off the tree. These he dropped down to

the children – one to each. 'Go straight on,' he said, 'straight along this path till you come to a huge rock. Walk round it! Keep hitting the rock with these twigs! As you do this you must each call upon it to open:

*Chanchassa Chanchassa Kilhiso!*
*I am the child of Masilo,*
*Open! Open!*

That's what you must say! You must go on doing this if nothing happens at first. If you only do it often enough, a door in the rock will have to fly open. When it does, go through, for inside is a place where you can live until you are grown up.'

The children took the twigs and started along the path. But they wondered if they would know which was the magic rock. Soon, however, there was no doubt about it, for they came in sight of an immense rock standing all by itself in the tall green grass, and the grass was the tallest and the rock the biggest that the children had ever seen. They walked round it calling out the words the bird had taught them:

*'Chanchassa Chanchassa Kilhiso!*
*I am the child of Masilo,*
*Open! Open!'*

Each time round they hit the rock with the magic twigs. Sure enough, after a time, a door in it did fly open and they looked in and saw that

inside was a huge cave. This cave was more beautifully furnished than
any hut they had ever seen. Oh, if only you could see it! It was so fine
that a great chief or a king might have lived in it. There were finely
plaited mats to sleep on, beautifully carved little wooden head-rests for
pillows, and splendid woven bedclothes and cloaks to keep the cold
away in the day. There were bright shell and bead necklaces and girdles
for Dumasine and, for each of them, a special cloak worked with beads.
For Duma, there was a bow and arrows, there was a long, curly koodoo
horn for him to blow, and beautiful small-sized throwing spears and
assegais. All round the walls of this wonderful place stood pots and
calabashes, each one dyed shining red and black. Some had cream in
them, some had fresh milk and some curds, or else delicious porridge
ready cooked. Besides all this there were three big closely woven baskets.
One was full of wheat, another was full of nuts, and a third full of maize.
They went in and, when they had looked all round, the children both
spoke together:

'This is the most beautiful place we have ever seen,' they said.
'Now we shall be quite happy!'

And there the two of them lived, till the boy had
become a fine young man and Dumasine the prettiest
young woman that you can imagine. There was
always plenty to eat, for the calabashes filled up again
as fast as Duma and Dumasine ate what was in them.
They taught themselves to cook and keep house, and
how to shoot the bow and arrows,
blow the koodoo horn and throw
the spears and assegais.

At last, one day, they found that
their food stores were getting low.
The calabashes and baskets were all
gradually getting empty and not
filling themselves up again.

'I know what it is. We are grown
up now and it is time we worked for

ourselves,' said the girl.

'Yes, let us go out into the world,' said the boy.

So they came out and after walking for many days they got back to the village where they had been born.

Their father and mother cried with joy when they saw that this fine young hunter and this lovely girl were none other than their lost Duma and Dumasine.

Every evening some of the people were sure to ask them to tell them their story – the very story that I've just told to you – and any stranger who came to the village was sure to want to hear

*The Tale of the Magic Bird.*

*There are many variations of this African story.
In one version, after the magic bird's escape,
there is the storm, but then all the children
disappear in a 'Pied Piper' incident. All, like
Duma and Dumasine, are then thoughtfully
looked after by various supernaturals, and return
to their parents as adults.*

*The children's names in this version are
Swazi and mean 'Children of Thunder'.*

# The Master
# Thief

LONG AGO, not in your day nor in my day, but in the very far
off days, an old couple, who were very poor, lived in a little
tumbledown cottage. One day a splendid carriage with four black horses
drew up to their door. As soon as it stopped, a richly dressed young

gentleman greeted the old couple politely, and asked them if they would be so kind as to let him stop to dinner with them. He added that, if they would agree, he would pay them well. The old people looked at each other, and then the old man answered that they were only poor folk and that, as usual, they had no food in the house that was fit to set before the gentry. But the stranger said that that was just what he had hoped, and that if they had some potatoes that would be enough dinner for him, for he had a special fancy for potato-balls, but that none of the grand cooks in any of the towns through which he had travelled knew how to make such things properly. So the end of it was that the old wife went into the kitchen, set on some water to heat, and began to peel and boil the potatoes, ready for making the potato-balls.

While she was busy over this, the old man and the strange gentleman strolled out into the orchard where the old man had already dug some holes ready to plant some new young apple trees. While the gentleman strolled about, the old man went on with his work. Soon the stranger began to watch him as, holding each young tree straight, he would fill in the hole and then tramp down the earth firmly round it. Then he would drive in a good stake beside each little tree and tie the young tree firmly to it with a straw rope.

'That's hard work for an old man like you,' said the strange gentleman. 'Haven't you got a son who could help you?'

'Well, sir, I did have a son,' answered the old man, leaning on his spade and sighing, 'but he was a wild contrary lad and never much good to me! He was sharp enough, but he never cared for work and at last he ran away from home, and now his mother and I don't know what has become of him.'

Presently the gentleman had another question. 'Why do you tramp down the earth round the roots of each of these young trees and then tie it to one of those upright stakes?'

The old man smiled, for he thought that great folk didn't know much about tree-planting.

'Why, sir,' said he, 'I do all that to make the roots firm and to make the trees grow straight! Trees must be trained while they're young.'

'Perhaps your son would have grown straight too,' answered the stranger, 'if you'd taken as much trouble rearing him as you do with your apple trees.'

At that the old man only shook his head and sighed again. Neither of them spoke for a while.

'Would you know your son if he should ever come back?' asked the stranger after a time.

'Ah,' said the old man, 'it's true enough that he'll have changed a good bit! For, of course, he was only a bit of a lad when he ran off, but even if he has changed, we should be bound to know him, for he has a little mark on his shoulder that looks just like a bean.'

'Come into the kitchen a minute,' said the stranger, and then, pulling off his coat and opening his shirt, he asked:

'Was the mark something like this?'

You can guess how astonished and delighted the old couple were to find that they had got their lost son back again and to find that he had become a grand gentleman. But they were not quite so delighted when he told them how it was that he had come to look like a lord and to be riding in a carriage drawn by four fine horses.

'When I left home,' said he, 'I fell in with a company of thieves and robbers, and soon I managed to do some work that surprised them.'

'What was that?' asked his mother.

'I managed to steal an ox as it was being driven to market, and then the next day, and the next, to steal two more oxen from the very same man and then to let him have his beasts again, and all without his ever finding out who had tricked him! I ended up by stealing all the robbers' horses – stealing them clean away from the thieves who thought they were teaching me! So after that, I knew I had learned my trade and so I set up on my own as a Master-Thief. Those robbers never dared do a thing to me, or to try to get their own back. They knew I could beat them at their own trade. So now I'm rich, and there are no locks or bolts that can keep me out. I just take anything I've a mind to. But don't be afraid! I never interfere with the likes of you! I only steal from rich people who have so much money they don't know what to do with it. Poor honest people haven't anything to fear!'

His father didn't like all this at all and he shook his head.

'No good ever came of such doings!' said the old man. But his wife said:

'Thief or no thief, he's still my son!' and when the Master-Thief had kissed his mother and given her a good hug, they all sat down to their dinner of potato-balls.

And now for a while they lived peaceably, with the Master-Thief sometimes lending a hand with the work and sometimes driving about in his fine carriage.

Now, not far from the cottage, in a very grand house, there lived a rich
nobleman, a Count, who had so much money that he couldn't tell how
much he had got. He had also got an only daughter and a smart and
pretty girl she was. On one of the days when he happened to be dressed
in his smart clothes and was out driving in his grand carriage with the
four black horses, the Master-Thief caught sight of the girl. He got out of
the carriage very politely and went over to speak to her and there he stood
with his hat in his hand, while they had a few words together. The end
of that was that they liked each other very well. He indeed liked the
Count's daughter so well that he soon determined that, somehow or
other, he would have her for his wife. So, the very next day, the Master-
Thief said to his father:

'I'd like you, if you please, Dad, to step up to the Great House
this morning.'

'What for?' asked his father.

'I just want you to ask the Count if I can marry his daughter,'
answered his son.

'You're out of your senses!' answered the old man.

'Nothing venture, nothing have!' said the Master-Thief.

'You can't be right in the head if you can talk such silly nonsense!'
answered his father. 'You just keep clear of the Count, or he's sure to
find out all about the life you've led and then it would be his job to get
you hanged for a thief!'

'I don't mind what he knows! You can be quite honest about it,
Dad!' answered his son, laughing. 'Just tell the Count straight out what
my trade is! But be sure to say that I'm not an ordinary thief, but a
Master-Thief.'

Well, you can guess that the poor old father didn't at all want to go
up to the Great House on an errand like that! However, his son gave
him no peace, so in the end, go he did. But when, at last, he actually
stood before the Count, the poor old fellow was trembling and almost
sobbing with fright.

'What's the matter with you, my man?' asked the Count.

At first the old man couldn't answer, but at last he told the Count the whole story – how his runaway son had come back looking like a grand gentleman; how he said he was a Master-Thief and how he now wanted to marry the Count's daughter.

But instead of being angry the Count only burst out laughing, and even patted the poor fellow on the back.

'Don't worry!' said the Count. 'We'll soon get the better of his impudence! Don't forget that if a man calls himself Master of any trade, he has got to show a Master-Piece – a really good job – for all the world to see! We'll make your young rascal show us three Master-Pieces – just because of his impudence! Never fear! I'll make them so hard that he'll never dare call himself a Master-Thief again! Just you send him along to me.'

Well, though he had heard the whole story, all the same the Count was rather surprised when a carriage with four black horses came up to the great house the next day and when such a grand and well-spoken young gentleman got out of it.

'So I hear that you fairly frightened your poor old father and that you told him that you're a Master-Thief?' said the Count.

At that the young man bowed politely.

'And what's more, I hear that you want to marry my daughter?'

The young man bowed again.

'I suppose you're willing to show me what you can do?' asked the Count.

'It will be a pleasure!' answered the Master-Thief.

'Well,' said the Count, looking very sly, 'just because of your impudence we'll see if you can do three Master-Pieces.'

'If it's thieving, Sir Count, I shall be delighted! Just say what they are!' answered the Master-Thief.

'First,' said the Count, 'you must try to steal my favourite mare from the stable.'

'Certainly.'

'But mind, I shall have a right to have her well guarded!'

'Oh, of course!' answered the young man. 'Guard her as much as you like!'

'Then, on Sunday morning, you must steal the joint that will be roasting for our Sunday dinner out of the kitchen under my very nose, and just when the cooks are busy basting it.'

'That won't be too hard,' answered the Master-Thief.

'And last of all,' went on the Count, looking slyer than ever, 'on Monday night you must steal the sheet off my bed and the nightgown that my wife will be wearing.'

'As you wish, Sir Count.'

'But don't forget,' added the Count, 'that if you can't do these three things, it's my business to

catch thieves and, what's more, to hang them!'

'Never mind about that,'

answered the Master-Thief pleasantly. 'But will you, on your side, promise that if I really can do all that, you'll let me marry your daughter – and no more questions asked?'

'Yes! On the word of a Count!' and with that they both laughed. The Count laughed because he was quite sure that nobody in the world would be able to trick him three times over. The Master-Thief laughed because he enjoyed doing that sort of thing and because he felt sure that he would be able to do all that and because the prize was a pretty wife who fancied him already.

So now, when they had taken leave of each other, they each began to make their preparations for the first trial. The Count arranged that six of his grooms should watch the mare in turns day and night, three by three. The first groom was to hold the mare's bridle, the second was to hold her tail, and the third was to sit on her back.

After he had warned the grooms, and seen them all in their places, the Count went off well pleased, quite sure that, even this first time, he had set the Master-Thief an impossible task. Indeed he believed that the impudent young fellow wouldn't even try, but would drive away in his grand carriage, and take his boasting tongue far away and so, like that, he would trouble them no more.

Meanwhile the Master-Thief really did drive off in his grand carriage! But he only went to the nearest town and, when he got there, he just did a little shopping. First he bought some second-hand clothes from an old peasant woman, then he got some brown stain, then he bought a nice little barrel, then some wine to put in it, and last of all he went to an old man in a by-street who sold all kinds of drugs and medicines, and giving him rather a strange prescription, he asked him to make up half a pint of the mixture.

'Half a pint?' said the old man, when he had read the prescription. 'It's powerful stuff, you know!'

'Yes, I know!' answered the Master-Thief.

Now, although it was coming on

to springtime, the nights were still cold, with a near frost, and when it got   *The Master Thief*
dark the three grooms (who had nothing to do except hold on to the
Count's favourite mare in a draughty stable) soon began to feel shivery.
It got colder and colder and quieter and quieter. Presently one of them
heard someone coughing outside.

'Who's there?' called out one of them.

'Only a poor old pedlar-woman!' answered a shrill voice from
the darkness.

The groom who was supposed to be holding the mare's tail took one
of the lanterns and went out to have a look. Sure enough, there sat an old
woman all crumpled up. She seemed to have been carrying a heavy load
on her back for there it was beside her, and she was coughing and
shivering pitifully in the darkness and cold.

'That's all it is,' said the groom when he came back to the others. 'Just
an old pedlar-woman! She says she's got no bed for the night and asked
me could she come in and lie down on the straw. It's just starting to sleet
outside! It's no night for a Christian to be out!'

The end of it was they let the old woman come in, and so in she
hobbled, and she seemed so bad with her cough that one of the grooms
had to help her with her burden. He noticed that the load seemed to be a
small wine-cask.

'What have you got in your cask, old lady?' one of them asked when
they'd had a good look at it in the light of the lanterns. But she seemed to
be so deaf that they had to ask her again.

'A nice mouthful of wine,' said the old woman at last, between
coughs. 'I get a living by peddling the stuff.'

'A little of that would soon
warm us up,' said the groom who
was sitting on the mare's back to the
others. Then he said:

'What would you take in
exchange for a glassful?'

'Money and good words,' said
the old woman.

So then he felt in his pocket and the other two grooms did the same, and, after a little bargaining, each of them bought a glassful. The wine was strong and soon began to warm them.

'When wine is good, I like a second glass!' said the groom who was holding on to the bridle.

'This wine really is old, I swear! It's as old as the old woman who sells it,' agreed the one who was upon the mare, and he reached down his glass for another fill, while the one who held the mare's tail soon put out his glass too. So it went on, and it wasn't long before

one groom decided that he could hold the mare's tail
every bit as well if he was sitting down, or even lying
down, while, as the bridle reins were long, the other
groom too had the same idea. So, as you can guess,
these two were soon fast asleep and snoring. And now,
somehow or other, the old woman seemed to have
stopped coughing and to be much more active than
before. Instead of hobbling she began to move about
quickly and busily, but keeping in the shadows.
Gently she loosed the hands that were still holding the
mare's tail and gently she put into their grasp a wisp of
straw instead, while the hands that had been holding
the reins soon had a piece of loose rope in them.

But now, what about the groom who still sat on the
mare's back? Peering up into his face the old woman
could see that he had noticed nothing because he was
sleeping as he sat. Nimbly the old dame unbuckled the
saddle girths, threw a couple of ropes over a beam that
was just above the mare's stall, tied the end of the ropes
to the saddle, and pulling hard on the free ends hoisted
the groom up, saddle and all, and made the ropes fast

to the posts of the stall. Who would have thought, half an hour earlier, that such a poor old woman with such a bad cough would have had the strength to do all that!

And now it was that the Master-Thief (for as you have already guessed, I'm sure, the old woman was none other) tucked up his petticoats, muffled the mare's feet by tying them up in old rags and, jumping nimbly on her back, rode her softly out of the stable. Out across the yard they went, and then, when they were well clear, he galloped her home to his father's stable.

It was when dawn was just breaking and when the Count was just getting up, and as he stood yawning and stretching as he looked out of his bedroom window, that the Master-Thief rode up on the stolen mare.

'Good morning, Sir Count!' called out the rider cheerfully. 'Here's your mare! Do go and look in the stable and see how comfortable your grooms are!'

Well, it was a lovely morning, the mare seemed none the worse, and the Master-Thief looked so cheerful that, though at first he felt vexed, the Count couldn't help bursting out laughing. Presently, when he came down and took over his mare again, he even clapped the Master-Thief on the back. But all the same, as he did so, he said to him:

'Don't make too sure, you young rascal, that you can just go on playing me tricks! No! Not even once more, let alone twice! Remember, tomorrow is Sunday! The Sunday one is going to be harder! However, you needn't try if you don't want to! You've still got time to use that fine carriage of yours.'

'Thank you very much for the warning, Sir Count,' said the Master-Thief and, this time, he pretended to look rather thoughtful, for, you see, he wanted the Count to think that perhaps he didn't mean to try the next thing, but would go off to where he came from.

As soon as he was out of sight and hearing, however, the Master-Thief began to whistle a cheerful tune. Off he walked to the village as fast as he could. There he managed to borrow a couple of hunting dogs, a net, and a sack, and then, with dogs, net and sack, he set off to the nearby mountain. By nightfall he had caught three hares, and had got them, all three safe and lively, in his sack. Then, once more whistling cheerfully, he returned the dogs and the net and went home with the three hares, very well pleased with himself, and had a good night's sleep.

Now, as the Count had reminded him, the next morning was Sunday. But though he meant to go to the Great House, the Master-Thief didn't put on his Sunday best. Not at all! He collected the oldest rags he could find and, where buttons were missing, he fastened these bits of clothes with odds and ends of string until he looked so poor and filthy that it made one's heart bleed to see him. Then, with his sack on his back, he stole into the passage at the back-door of the Count's house, just like any other beggar. The Count himself and all his household were in the kitchen, watching the roast. Just as they were most busy, the Master-Thief let one of the hares out of the sack, and it set off tearing round and round the yard in front of the kitchen's windows.

'Oh, just look at that hare!' said the folks in the kitchen, and several of them were all for running out to catch it. Yes, the Count too saw it running.

'Oh, let it run,' said he. 'There's no use in thinking to catch a hare in the spring!'

It wasn't long before the hare found a way to get out and disappeared.

A while afterwards, the Master-Thief let the second hare go, and again they saw it from the kitchen. They all thought it must be the same hare that they had seen before, and now more of them wanted to run out and catch a March Hare, but at last this hare also managed to find a way out.

It was not long before the Master-Thief let the third hare go, and this one too set off and began to run round and round the kitchen-yard, exactly as the others had done before it. And still they all thought it must be the same hare that kept on running about, and everyone of them was eager to be out after it.

'Well, it's certainly a fine hare!' agreed the Count at last. 'And it doesn't seem to know how to get out either. All right, let's see if we can't get it!'

So out he ran, and the rest with him – away they all went, the hare

before, and they after; so it was rare fun to see. But the Master-Thief didn't waste time watching. Indeed, he snatched up the roast and ran off with it; and where the Count got a roast for dinner that day I don't know; but one thing I do know, and that is, that he didn't manage to get a hare to roast, though he ran after it till he was both warm and weary. That was twice he had been tricked!

So now, if the Count kept his word, there was only one more master-piece of thieving that had to be done before there could be a wedding. This was Monday's task, and what the Master-Thief had to do was to steal the sheet off the Count's own bed, and the nightgown that the Countess his wife would be wearing.

As they had done before, the Count and the Master-Thief each began their preparations. The Master-Thief waited till it was dark; then he went to the gallows; there he found a poor dead prisoner hanging. He carried the body on his back to the Great House and hid it among the trees in the garden. After that he went and fetched a ladder which would be long enough to reach up to the Count's bedroom window. As for the Count, what he did was to get a musket, load it, lay it by his bedside and go to sleep.

Presently, when the moon was up, the Master-Thief got his ladder, set it up very quietly, and then with the dead man on his back, he climbed up it. He climbed just high enough for the head of the dead man to show at the window. Then he made a bit of a noise, and he kept bobbing it up and down so that it looked for all the world like someone peeping in. The Count woke up.

'There's the Master-Thief,' whispered he to his wife, giving her a

nudge. 'Now you watch me shoot him,' and with that he took up the musket.

'Oh, don't shoot him after telling him he might come and try,' whispered his wife.

'I'll shoot him all right!' replied the Count, and he took good aim. Next time the head popped up – *bang!* The Count had shot the body of the dead hanged prisoner right through the head.

The Master-Thief, who of course had kept well out of musket-shot, immediately let the body go. Down it fell, down to the foot of the ladder, landing with a thump. As quietly and quickly as the wind, the Master-Thief ran down the ladder and hid among the bushes, while the Count, getting quickly out of bed, leaned out of the window. Sure enough there was a dead body lying on the ground.

Then the Count began to scratch his head.

'It is quite true,' said he to his wife, 'that I am the chief magistrate in these parts and that the Master-Thief had done plenty of crimes. But people are fond of talking and maybe they'll wonder why we didn't have a trial and all that. I believe the best thing will be for me just to go down and bury him quietly. So don't you say a word about it!'

'You must do as you think best, dear,' answered his wife.

So now, down the ladder went the Count. He shouldered the body of the poor prisoner, and, taking a spade, he went off to a secret place in the garden.

No sooner had he gone and had begun to dig a grave, than the Master-Thief said to himself:

'Now's the time!' Up the ladder he climbed and in through the window and was soon in the bedroom. It was much darker in there than out in the moonlight.

'Why, dear, back already?' said the Countess, seeing a man standing there and thinking that it was her husband.

'Why yes,' said the Master-Thief, in a very good imitation of the Count's voice. 'I just put him into a hole and threw a little earth over him. But just let me have the sheet to wipe myself with – he was all covered with blood and I have made myself in such a mess with him!'

So that is how the Master-Thief got the sheet!

Then he went to the darkest corner of the room, and pretended to be busy with it. After a while he said:

'Do you know I am afraid you will have to let me have your nightgown too. I'm in such a mess! The sheet won't get it all off!' So the Countess took off her nightgown and gave it to him. But now the Master-Thief had to think of an excuse to get away.

'Do you know, dear wife,' said he, 'I believe I must have left one of his feet sticking out! That will never do! To make my mind easy I'll go down and make sure before I go back to bed again,' and then off he went down the ladder and with him he took both the sheet and the nightgown.

He was only just in time, for now the real Count had finished burying the poor prisoner. Up the ladder he came and into the room.

'Had you really left one of his feet sticking out?' asked the Countess. 'And what have you done with the sheet and with my nightgown?'

'What's that?' called out the Count.

'Why, dear! I'm only asking you what you've done with the sheet and with my nightgown! You used them to wipe off the blood,' said she.

Well, though they talked till it was morning, neither of them could make out what it was that had happened.

However, once daylight came, they had not much longer to wait, for they were hardly up and dressed when there before them stood the Master-Thief, and what is more, there stood their pretty daughter with him.

Well, as you know, the Count and Countess were the sort that can take a joke, and though the Countess felt a bit nervous as to what sort of husband her daughter was going to have, they had to agree to the marriage, for the Count had given his word. So now the two young people knelt before them and got their blessing. To tell the truth the Count wouldn't have dared refuse him now, for he was almost afraid that his new son-in-law would steal everything that he had, daughter included, if he did anything to vex him.

And that was how it was that the Master-Thief became the son-in-

law to a Count, and how he became
a rich man, and how he got a pretty
wife who loved him. I don't know
whether he ever stole any more, but
I am sure, if he did, it was just for a
bit of fun and that he gave back
whatever he stole.

*A German tale*

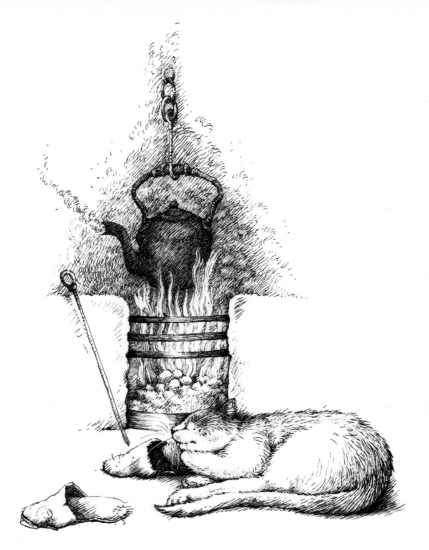

# White-Faced Siminy

I N OLDEN TIMES, when a girl wanted a place as a servant, off
she would go to a hiring-fair.

Well, one day, there was a young farm-girl who wanted a place, so off
she went to the fair like the rest. She stood with the others and each one
had a posy of flowers to show that they were all seeking a new place.

One girl was hired and another was hired, but there she stood. At last, towards evening, a funny-looking little old man came along, hired the farm-girl and off they went to his house.

He seemed a nice fellow and they had supper together. Afterwards, while they were sitting beside the fire, he told her that in his house he expected the servant to call things by their proper names.

'What would you call me, for instance?' said he.

'Master, or mister, or whatever you please, sir,' said she.

'No,' said he, 'you must call me *Don Nippery Septo*. And what would you call these?' said he pointing to his shoes.

'Slippers, or shoes, or whatever you please, sir.'

'You must call them *hay-down treaders*, my dear. And what would you call these?' He pointed to his trousers.

'Breeches, or bags, or whatever you please, sir.'

'No, you must call them *fortune's crackers*. And what's this?' said he, pointing to the staircase.

'Steps or stairs, or whatever you please, sir.'

'Not a bit of it, my girl! That's the *wooden hill* and up there is my *barnacle*,' he said, pointing to where his bed was, up above. 'And what would you call her, now?' asked he, as he stroked the cat.

'Cat, or Kit, or whatever you please, sir.'

'No, no! You must call her *White-Faced Siminy*. And this here?' and he pointed at the fire.

'Fire, or heat, or whatever you please, sir.'

'Dear me, no! It's *hot cockolorum*. And what is this?' He showed her what was in the bucket.

'Water, or wet, or whatever you please, sir.'

'Not at all! That's *pondolorum*. And what would you call this?' said he, pointing to the house.

'Cottage, or house, or whatever you please, sir.'

'No! No! *Great Castle of Strawbungle* is its name.'

That very night, the girl, in a fright, woke up her master and this is what she said:

'DON NIPPERY SEPTO! Get out of your BARNACLE and put on your

HAY-DOWN TREADERS and your FORTUNE'S
CRACKERS. Come down the WOODEN HILL as fast
as you can, for WHITE-FACED SIMINY has got a spark
of HOT COCKOLORUM on her tail and unless we get some more
PONDOLORUM, the GREAT CASTLE OF STRAWBUNGLE will soon be
all on HOT COCKOLORUM!.

*An English tale*